Margaret Wise Brown
illustrated by Ashley Wolff

LITTLE
DONKEY
CLOSE
YOUR
EYES

HARPERCOLLINSPUBLISHERS

Little Donkey Close Your Eyes
Text copyright © 1959 by William R. Scott, Inc.,
renewed 1987 by Roberta Brown Rauch.
Illustrations copyright © 1995 by Ashley Wolff
Printed in Mexico. All rights reserved.

Library of Congress Cataloging-in-Publication Data
Brown, Margaret Wise, 1910–1952.
    Little Donkey close your eyes / Margaret Wise Brown ; illustrated by
Ashley Wolff.
        p.   cm.
    Summary: As the day comes to a close, various animals and a small
child wind down their activities and go to sleep.
    ISBN 0-06-024482-8. — ISBN 0-06-024483-6 (lib. bdg.)
    [1. Sleep—Fiction.   2. Bedtime—Fiction.   3. Animals—Fiction.
4. Stories in rhyme.]   I. Wolff, Ashley, ill.   II. Title.
PZ8.3.B815Lj   1995   <Rare Bk Coll>
[E]—dc20   94-16523
                                                                CIP
                                                                 AC

Typography by Al Cetta
1   2   3   4   5   6   7   8   9   10
❖
First Edition

For Brennan and Rowan, with love

—A.W.

Little Donkey
on the hill
Standing there
so very still

Making faces
at the skies
Little Donkey
close your eyes.

Little Monkey
in the tree
Swinging there
so merrily

Throwing coconuts
at the skies
Little Monkey
close your eyes.

Silly Sheep
that slowly crop
Night has come
and you must stop

Chewing grass
beneath the skies
Silly Sheep
now close your eyes.

Little Pig
that squeals about
Make no noises
with your snout

No more squealing
to the skies
Little Pig
now close your eyes.

Wild young birds
that sweetly sing
Curve your heads
beneath your wing

Dark night covers
all the skies
Wild young birds
now close your eyes.

Old black cat
down in the barn
Keeping five
small kittens warm

Let the wind
blow in the skies
Dear old black cat
close your eyes.

Little child
all tucked in bed
Looking such
a sleepy head

Stars are quiet
in the skies
Little child
now close your eyes.